THE LITTLE MERMAID

HANS CHRISTIAN ANDERSEN, 1805-1875

Oil painting by C. A. Jensen, 1836

THE LITTLE MERMAID

by

Hans Christian Andersen

WITH AN INTRODUCTION

by ERIK DAL

TRANSLATED BY DAVID HOHNEN

Høst & Søn
COPENHAGEN

© *Høst & Søns Forlag, Copenhagen 1959*
Printed in Denmark by J. H. Schultz Bogtrykkeri, Copenhagen
Cover by Inga Aistrup
4th revised edition printed in offset by
S. L. Møllers Bogtrykkeri, Copenhagen 1964

DEN LILLE HAVFRUE was first printed in *Eventyr fortalte for Børn*, 3. Hæfte, 1837. The author invariably signed his name H. C. Andersen except in letters to English friends from 1848-49 onwards, in which he wrote it out in full:
HANS CHRISTIAN ANDERSEN.

Introduction

Hans Christian Andersen had just completed his thirtieth year when, in April and May of 1835, he published two works: a long novel entitled *The Improvisatore* (Improvisatoren), which reflected parts of his own life and his travels in Italy; and the first instalment of his *Tales for Children* (Eventyr fortalte for Børn). At this time he already had quite an extensive output behind him, works of varying merit that today would only be known to specialists were it not for the fact that their author's subsequent career has made us wise after the event. His career up to this time had already been unusual. Hans Christian Andersen's father was a cobbler in Odense on the island of Funen, and a fanciful dreamer; his lanky son had experienced many weird things before finally leaving his proletarian environments in order to seek his fortune in Copenhagen. This was in 1819. Denmark's capital with its 100,000 inhabitants was cramped in behind the old fortification ramparts. But, despite its provinciality and impoverishment following the English bombardment of 1807 and the state bankruptcy of 1813, Copenhagen managed to foster a period of literary activity since known in the Danish literature as the Golden Age; it likewise provided a creative atmosphere for a number of personalities of international standing, such as H. C. Ørsted, discoverer of electro-magnetism, N. F. S. Grundtvig, composer of hymns and conceiver of the Folk High School movement, and later for the philosopher, Søren Kierkegaard, and the sculptor, Bertel Thorvaldsen, after his return from Italy.

Just why leading personalities in the intellectual life and administration of this little community should have taken the poor, stranded lad under their wings when he was struggling to become a ballet-dancer or an opera-singer, will never be fully clarified. Something about him – perhaps his eyes, or his voice? – must have revealed hidden values behind his unorthodox appearance and odd behaviour. The fact remains that his early benefactors enabled him to complete secondary school, and later on he met with goodwill and friendship from many quarters. During his younger years this was of great importance financially, and throughout life it remained a necessity to this sensitive, unmarried and, from a human viewpoint, by no means entirely attractive writer.

He never settled down. Rented lodgings (and for many years rented furniture too), regular visits to the home of a civil servant, Jonas Collin, and to other Copenhagen friends, countless stays at Danish country manors, and in addition, travels abroad of a scope rarely paralleled in his day (even as far as Constantinople and Algiers) – thus the life of this lonely man. Titles, decorations, a solid banking account and real fame, all were his as the years passed; but it does not alter our impression of the outer and inner restlessness that prevailed during the seventy years he lived.

He continued writing until his death, and tried his hand at most forms, novels and travel-books constituting the solid core of his production; he wrote poems of many kinds, a great number of dramatic works and auto-biographical studies, and – what must be included amongst his literary bequest to mankind – an extensive correspondence of great value; the lengthier exchanges have been published in our time. The percentage of waste in his production is large; there is something particularly tragi-comical about the eagerness with which this author of inspired tales wooed the muses of the theatre. None of his plays has survived. In the passage of time his poems and songs have been subjected to a process of critical

6

selectivity. While some of them are really astonishingly bad. a few are implanted in the heart of every Dane just as early in life, and just as deeply, as the tales.

However, nobody would wish to dispute the fact that the tales, and the tales alone (or some of them) subsequently were responsible for the world renown with which we like to associate Hans Christian Andersen's name. Even in Denmark, a more extensive reading of Andersen's other works is something only for those especially interested; admittedly such persons are not few in number.

THE TALE

That *The Improvisatore* is a work worth reading for its own sake is apparent from the many translations that were made within a few years after it was first published, and no less by reason of the fact that, as recently as in 1931, it was translated into the language of the country under whose skies it was conceived. Such a lengthy and picturesque novel was indeed a worthy gesture in return for the travelling funds made available to the author and marks the real turning-point in his career as well. It was only H. C. Ørsted, the physicist, who appreciated the inner potentialities of the two books published in the spring of 1835. "I have then written," announced Andersen in a letter dated March 16, 1835, to his faithful friend Henriette Wulff, "some tales for children; Ørsted says about them that if *The Improvisatore* makes me famous, these tales will make me immortal, and that they are the most perfect things I have written. But I don't think so. He doesn't know Italy, and so cannot rejoice at the familiar breezes that float up from the pages of the book towards him." (And, one might add, was for this reason a more objective judge than the travel-happy author himself!)

Andersen can hardly have harboured the idea of publishing the tales any length of time. He had attempted tales on a couple of previous occasions, but in his normal style which was that of the literature of his day. The novelty did not lie in his powers of invention (for some of the earliest of his tales are based on folk tales, absorbed traditionally by word of mouth in his childhood surroundings on the island of Funen) but in his intention: while *told for children,* the tales were intended at the same time as reading matter for grown-ups – and indeed in many respects extend far beyond the horizon of a child. The first indication of the plan we find in a letter to the Danish authoress Henriette Hanck, dated January 1, 1835: "I am now starting on some 'tales for children'. I intend to win the coming generations, you see!" On March 26, 1835, the completed, unpublished manuscript is spoken of as "... the work of my immortality! Of course I shan't enjoy the experience in this world." There is pride as well as self-irony in these remarks. On February 10, 1835, in similarly cheerful tones, he informed his somewhat older friend, the author B. S. Ingemann, of his plan: "... I have written them exactly the way I should tell them to *a child.*"

This was the point. This was the novelty. Never before had the Danish language been recorded as candidly and ingeniously as in these tales. This was not only how children in particular spoke and thought, but also the way ordinary, non-academic people used the language. The whimsical transitions of speech, the small words that are so alive, the unmisunderstandable breaches in logic – all these were ingredients in what was in addition poetic prose of great breadth of expression. Surprise, even indignation, were the immediate reactions – what a step backward after *The Improvisatore!* Nevertheless, the Danish language was to be influenced by these tales for all time. In so saying, we must concede that it is not only due to over-educationalistic, over-literary, or merely incompetent or mercantile translators that this unique form of life was not allowed to blossom in very many of the translations

8

subsequently made. It is also due to the fact that here we find ourselves listening to the most intimate shades of meaning our language has to offer, shades so fine that even the best translators often have given up trying to grasp, or at all events reproduce, the full combination of overtones in the unmistakable soughing of the conch-shell.

The Little Mermaid is not one of the tales that presents particular linguistic problems; unfortunately the serious diction of this long fairy-tale contains but few examples of Andersenian whimsicality. The tale ranked high in his own estimation and in that of his contemporaries. Together with *The Emperor's New Clothes* (Kejserens nye Klæder) it constituted the third instalment of the tales, which appeared on May 7, 1837. Although it is an original story and not an elaboration of a folk tale, it has roots in Andersen's earlier production and moreover in the literature of his times.

Danish romanticism had accepted traditional concepts of mermaids from older literature, partly from Danish folk ballads, partly from antique and oriental prototypes, and partly from German romanticism, Fouqué's *Undine* in particular. By reason of her particular fate – that of literally being half human – the mermaid was interpreted, with varying tones of eroticism, at one moment as being non-human, the powerful and prophetic representative of vice and heathen nature, and the next as being almost human, as one longing for release and salvation. According to a well-known passage in the Bible (The Epistle of St. Paul to the Romans, Chap. VIII), Nature knows this longing; but the particular opportunity supernatural beings might enjoy, of being released by the love of a human being, is genuine folklore. It is this folkloristic interpretation which has been incorporated, using the palest possible shades of eroticism, in Hans Christian Andersen's fairy-tale, which was based on Ingemann's *Creatures of the*

Underworld (De Underjordiske) and folk ballads. But whilst Ingemann's tale ends happily, Andersen's, in accordance with the whole course of events, has to end with the death of the little mermaid. He has fought shy of this solution and, by means of the "daughters of the air" ("sort of welfare home sylphs" as they have been called) of his own invention, given the tale a 'sloppy' ending, which, in an unfortunate manner, serves to lengthen the threads of sentimentality interwoven throughout this otherwise beautiful story. The facsimile of the manuscript reproduced on page 20 shows that a further belabouring of this ending was finally deleted with praiseworthy, albeit insufficient, determination.

The mermaid theme had, however, already been used by H. C. Andersen prior to 1836, on one occasion in a play written only a few years earlier. By using a currently popular theme Andersen apparently felt he was able to insert actual emotions and moods: a recently renewed acquaintance with childhood regions that seemed far away, isolated just as though on the bottom of the sea, and a restlessly dissatisfied yearning back and forth between two poles – a romantic, but at the same time deeply personal emotion; it is reflected in the play, but in the fairy-tale it has been replaced by a more determined striving towards a goal, that of eternal life. The personal history of the whole tale has been interpreted by Professor Hans Brix in this way: the little mermaid's unrequited love for the prince represents the author's love for Louise, the daughter of his benefactor Jonas Collin, and all that this connection could mean to Andersen. The bottom of the sea is the world from which he came, and the dry land above that in which he sought to obtain citizenship. And Louise's love in return, which would create for him a place in the home and a status of fraternal equality towards his friend Edvard Collin, is the objective for which the struggle is being made, but not attained – the whole narrative being adorned with the bright and splendid colours of the south. Mute adoration is met with goodness and kindness as long as it lasts, but with no more.

Correspondence with Henriette Hanck would appear to show that our fairy-tale was planned – at latest – at the beginning of 1836, and that it was first given the title of *Daughters of the Air* (Luftens Døtre). On May 13, 1836, Andersen mentioned that the composition of *Daughters of the Sea* (!) was imminent and easily accomplished. By January 23, 1837, the manuscript was completed, and shortly before its publication the following delightful exchange took place in letters to and from Miss Hanck, and dated March 9, and March 30, 1837, respectively.

From Andersen:

"My tales are going to be published at the same time. They comprise The Little Mermaid, which is definitely good, and The Emperor's New Clothes. My love to [your] little [private pupil] Bertha, and tell her mermaids can't be called Bertha, otherwise I would have given the little mermaid that name."

And from Miss Hanck:

"By now I am sure the third instalment of your tales will have appeared. When it comes to town I shall look forward to reading it to the children; they have, like most children, such a lively feeling and pure taste for all that is beautiful, that I respect their opinion of your little book just as much as that of most grown-ups."

H. C. Andersen, who was not the kind of author that is always best pleased with his most recent work, was not disappointed in his confidence in *The Little Mermaid*'s merits, and it would in fact be ungenerous if one allowed oneself to harbour the suspicion today, that its success has been due in part to the fact that this tale, in its language and theme, is less strikingly novel than some of the earlier tales. In his interesting observations concerning the tales, at the end of Chapter X in *The Story of my Life* (Mit Livs Eventyr), Andersen stresses the fact that "by this tale in particular attention was aroused"; and his brief notes accompanying the edition of the tales published in 1862 reveal that *The Little Mermaid* "aroused much attention and encouraged me to invent myself" – Andersen had until then used more borrowed themes than original for his fairy-tales. On February 15, 1841, Henriette Hanck, in reply to a despondent letter, had to make reference to the unanimous favour which this tale had won. And many years later, as he reveals in a letter to Henriette Collin dated July 1, 1858, Andersen happened to find himself travelling in a diligence together with a Frenchman who was reading the story on his journey.

Other evidence of the significance and the impact of the tale could be produced, but we may close here with an excerpt from a letter addressed to B. S. Ingemann, dated February 11, 1837. This contains some observations of importance concerning H. C. Andersen and his tales, and about *The Little Mermaid* in particular.

"At the earliest opportunity you shall receive a new instalment of children's tales – which of course you don't care for. Heiberg says they are the best I have written. The latest tale, "The Little Mermaid", you *will* like; it is better than Thumbelina [Tommelise] and is, except for The Little Abbess's Story [Den lille Abbedisses Historie] in The Improvisatore the only one of my works that has affected me while I was writing it. You smile, perhaps? Well now, I don't know how other writers feel! *I* suffer with my characters, I share their humours, whether good or bad, and I can be nice or nasty according to the scene on which I happen to be working. This latest, third instalment of tales for children is probably the best, and you're going to like it! Yes, your wife will like it very much! I have not, like de la Motte Fouqué in Undine, allowed the mermaid's acquiring of an immortal soul to depend upon an alien creature, upon the love of a human being. I'm sure that's wrong! It would depend rather much on chance, wouldn't it? I *won't* accept that sort of thing in this world. I have permitted my mermaid to follow a more natural, more divine path. No other writer, I believe, has indicated it yet, and that's why I am glad to have it in my tale. You'll see for yourself!"

THE ILLUSTRATIONS

The Little Mermaid has had the same fate as so many of Hans Christian Andersen's tales and stories, namely that of achieving world fame in translations into a considerable number of the ninety languages in which Andersen is known to be represented today. Germany was the first foreign country to accept and illustrate the tales (see G. Osterwald's drawing on page 36). England followed suit, and an etching of the mermaid's visit to the sea-witch was the first of all English Andersen illustrations (page 45). Lady Duff-Gordon was responsible for the translation, and Andersen himself was her guest during his eventful trip to England in 1847. Later on, translations were made into the languages of the other major countries. But fame carried with it a disadvantage. The translations were often poor, and abridgements for miniature editions and painting-books gave but a crude outline of the author's intentions. Thus today, conscientious translators and literary experts experience difficulty in making it clear to an interested reading public that Hans Christian Andersen is not merely a semi-anonymous teller of fairy-tales for the nursery, but a great Danish author having an appeal to young and old alike. Here however, we shall rest content with observing the distribution of his work, not only throughout Europe but also to foreign continents. Some of the other tales, especially some of the shorter ones, have enjoyed even greater distribution; but so have lengthier tales like *The Wild Swans* (De vilde Svaner) and *The Snow Queen* (Snedronningen). *The Little Mermaid,* however, is quite definitely one of the tales that have served to establish their author's fame far and wide. Dramatizations and other free adaptations have been made from it – in fact even a German opera.

Illustrators naturally followed the translators. Despite the fact, as already indicated, that other tales may be more widely known, and also no doubt have had a greater appeal to the imaginations of artists, hundreds of drawings illustrating *The Little Mermaid,* originating in Europe – and in a few other places – are also to be encountered. The quality of such illustrations likewise varies considerably, partly in regard to time and place, and partly in regard to the basic approach of each individual artist to the tales themselves. Danes will doubtless find many of the attempts on the part of foreign artists very much on the cheaply facile side, in the traditional "fairytale" style, or, alternatively, overdramatized and bombastic. In this edition, however, an endeavour has been made to bring together a representative selection of Danish and foreign illustrations to the tale, ranging from the earliest of all the Andersen illustrations right up until the year 1959, and embracing ten European countries as well as the USA, Japan, and China. Naively childish or technically sophisticated, dramatic or intimate, all manner of interpretations are to be found here side by side. And if we find ourselves looking in vain for that humour which otherwise characterizes a number of Andersen's best tales, the artists are not to be blamed; the humour just happens to be missing in this one. The source of each illustration is given at the end of the book; a number of the illustrations, e. g. Vilhelm Pedersen's, Yan' Dargent's and A. Rackham's, have gone round most of the world in the form of re-reproductions in new editions and translations.

In Denmark, the work of two illustrators, Vilhelm Pedersen and Lorenz Frølich, is regarded as classic, despite the fact that occasionally genuine attempts at new illustrative interpretation have been made in the author's own country too. Our present tale is in a unique position with regard to these two illustrators. Vilhelm Pedersen (who was a lieutenant in the navy as well as an artist) managed to illustrate, between 1848 and his untimely death in 1859, all the tales and stories dating from this period, which include practically all the best known ones. It was Hans Christian Andersen who had recommended him for the task (set by the Danish-born German publisher, Carl B. Lorck) and similarly it would appear to be Andersen who, in the 1860's, caused Lorenz Frølich to take up the thread and illustrate his later work. Foreigners must accept the fact that Danes will always tend to see the tales the way the sensitive and intimate Vilhelm Pedersen, or the more satirical and imaginative Lorenz Frølich, saw them; no artist, these two not excepted, has ever been able to complement Andersen entirely in richness and multiplicity of expression.

But the unique thing about *The Little Mermaid* is that it has been illustrated twice by Lorenz Frølich as well as by Vilhelm Pedersen. Of the latter's four classical drawings, two are reproduced in this edition, on pages 23 and 51. At the age of seventeen, Frølich executed eleven simple and graceful drawings to illustrate the newly published tale; Andersen knew and appreciated this series, but it has only recently been made known to the public in its entirety (see page 26). And at the age of 83, almost 70 years after his little youthful achievement, and more than 50 years after Pedersen's work, Frølich undertook the task of illustrating this and two other tales for a fine quarto edition bearing the title of *Three Tales* (Tre Eventyr), published in 1905 to commemorate the centenary of Andersen's birth. On this occasion the old master made some twenty large, full-page drawings in pen-and-ink, splendidly and boldly executed from a point of view of imagination as well as technique, and returned in this manner to woo an old love. But this series is not very well known in Denmark either.

THE STATUE

That *The Little Mermaid* however, should occupy such a prominent place in the minds of many foreigners is not due solely to the fairy-tale itself and its illustrators, but just as much to the fact that it is associated with the well-known statue of The Little Mermaid in Copenhagen. This is situated on Langelinie, Copenhagen's beautiful and popular harbour mole promenade where the moats and ramparts of The Citadel, eastern defence post of the old city fortifications, extend out to the Sound. It lies to the south of the big free port, and to the northeast of the central parts of the city and the harbour; on the jacket of this book the statue is shown against a background of the big factory buildings and dockyards situated on the islands in the waters between Zealand and the island of Amager.

The Langelinie terrain has provided sites for a number of different works of art, and in 1913, *Edvard Eriksen*'s bronze statue of a mermaid was set up on a lump of rock by the waterside as a gift from Carl Jacobsen, a well-known brewer and patron of the arts. Edvard Eriksen (1876–1959) executed, before as well as after 1913, a number of much-praised works of sculpture, among them the sarcophagus and monument of Christian IX and Queen Louise in Roskilde Cathedral. Moreover, he was active as a teacher at the Royal Academy of Fine Arts, and as a restorer at Thorvaldsen's Museum. Fate has accorded his bronze mermaid a special place in his life-work, and one can hardly be accused of detracting from his memory if one claims that his work, like much

16

good folk art, lives in the minds of many without his name being known.

Carl Jacobsen was inspired to make his gift after watching Ellen Price, a Danish ballerina, dance a ballet composed on the theme of *The Little Mermaid* to music by Fini Henriques. For a time the dancer herself is said to have sat for the sculptor as his model ("only partly", as one encyclopaedia points out; this reservation, however, has been made out of deference, not to the mermaid's shape, which, incidentally, is more human than in the tale, but to the fact that the only real model was Mrs. Edvard Eriksen). Ellen Price, as it happens, was a great-grand-child of Hans Christian Andersen's fatherly friend, Jonas Collin. When the setting up of the statue had been cele-brated by a banquet at Carl Jacobsen's home, the whole company drove out to have at look at it, whereupon the brewer suddenly dragged forth a length of hose from his car, sprayed the statue, and said: "Now you can see what she looks like when she's wet!" – a startling but really very reasonable impulse.

The statue's popularity has naturally quite a lot to do with the fact that it is no longer regarded as a work of art, but as a symbol, and if the occasional sober-minded tourist should happen to find himself disappointed at the sight, he must console himself with the fact that the famous little girl is at any rate prettier to behold than a no less well-known and – in its way – equally wet statue of a boy in Brussels. And not only do Danish and foreign tourists throng round, from morn till night, photograph-ing and being photographed and falling into the water, but seafaring folk come to pay the statue a visit too, for she is said to bring good luck. It is claimed that Dutch and Brazilian sailors regard it as being lucky to have kissed the little mermaid in the port of Copenhagen.

It can hardly be the task of a Dane to explain to foreigners what foreigners see in Edvard Eriksen's little statue, and what it symbolizes for them. But it seems as though they, boldly disregarding many important characteristics, like to consider Denmark, Hans Christian Andersen and The Little Mermaid as being a happy triad, symbolic of an idyllic fairyland. And we shall doubtless have to grant them that this is what our country and its most universal writer are like – as well!

———————

Most readers will appreciate that this introduction, in the majority of respects, has relied upon the many monographs and annotated editions of Hans Christian Andersen. This is not the place for a bibliography, but the editor would like to acknowledge, with gratitude, his indebtedness, in particular to Professor, Dr. Hans Brix (especially for his thesis on H. C. Andersen and his Tales, 1907), to Mr. Svend Larsen, curator of the H. C. Andersen House at Odense (especially for his edition of the Henriette Hanck correspondence), and above all, to Dr. H. Topsøe-Jensen, senior librarian at the University Library, Copenhagen (especially for his editions of the Henriette Wulff correspondence and of *The Story of My Life*).

The facsimile of the last page of the fairy-tale reproduced on page 20 from the original manuscript, together with the transcription on p. 19, should serve to give an impression of three things: H. C. Andersen's handwriting, his prose, and his method of working. The manuscript was discovered by chance in a French second-hand bookshop as recently as in 1920 and is now the property of the H. C. Andersen House at Odense, which has published a complete facsimile edition supplying the text in English as well as in Danish; the cliché for this facsimile page has kindly been lent by the publishers. The Danish text is printed below; the words which have been crossed out are indicated by square brackets in the Danish text and their translation is given in footnotes at the bottom of the page.

(Og den lille Havfrue løftede sine klare Arme op mod) Guds Sol og for første Gang følte hun Taarer [strømme ud af fra sine Øine][1]. Paa Skibet var igjen Støi og Liv, hun saae

Prindsen med sin smukke Brud, søge efter hende, [og]² vee-
modigt stirre de paa det boblende Skum, som om de vidste
hun havde styrtet sig (i) Bølgerne. [Og]³ Usynlig kyssede hun
Brudens Pande, smiilte til *ham* og steeg med de andre Luftens Børn op paa den rosenrøde Sky, som seilede i Luften.
»Om trehundrede Aar svæve vi saaledes ind i Guds Rige!«
[som straaler langt herligere end Solen, som kun er en Gnist]⁴
sagde de,
    »[dog]⁵ Ogsaa tidligere kunne vi komme der hvidskede een.
»Usynligt svæve vi [gjennem]⁶ ind i Menneskenes Huse, hvor
der er Børn og for hver Dag vi [finde tre gode B]⁷ finde eet
godt Barn, som gjør sine Forældre Glæde og fortjener deres
Kjærlighed forkorter Gud vor Prøvetid; Barnet veed ikke
naar vi flyve gjennem Stuen og maa vi da af Glæde smile
over det, da [forkortes]⁸ tages et Aar fra de trehundrede, men
see vi et uartigt og ondt Barn da maa vi græde Sorgens
Graad og hver Taare lægger en Dag til i vor Prøve Tid!«
[Selv vil jeg stræbe efter at vinde en udødelig Sjæl, sagde
den lille Havfrue, da skal jeg i hiin Verden samles med
[Prindsen og alle] ham, som jeg gav min hele Kjærlighed.
Til Rige og Fattiges Huus vil jeg flyve, svæve usynlig gjennem Stuen hvor Børnene sidde, de gode jeg møder ville for-
korte min Prøvetid!« –]⁹   endt den 23. Jan. 37.

1: streaming out from her eyes 2: and 3: And 4: which
shines much more splendidly than the sun, which is only a
spark 5: But 6: through 7: find three good children (NB. The
Danish word Børn, meaning children, was abbreviated) 8: will
be shortened 9: I myself will strive to win an immortal soul,
said the little mermaid, when I join, in yonder world, (the
prince and all) him to whom I gave all my love. Into the
houses of rich and poor will I fly, float invisibly through the
room where the children are sitting; the good ones I meet will
shorten my period of trial!

The Little Mermaid

Far out at sea, the water is as blue as the petals on the fairest cornflower, and as clear as the purest glass; but it is very deep, deeper than any anchorline can go, and many church towers would have to be placed one on top of the other to reach from the bottom up to the surface. Down there live the sea people.

Now you must not think there is nothing but the bare, white, sandy bottom. No, there are the strangest plants and trees, whose stalks and leaves are so supple that at the slightest movement in the water, they move, just as if they were alive. All the fishes, great and small, flit amongst the branches, just like the birds up here in the air. At the very deepest place is the sea king's palace, the walls of which are made of coral, and the long, pointed windows of the clearest amber; but the roof is of mussel shells that open and close with the swirl of the water. It looks very pretty, for in each shell lie shining pearls; one alone would be splendid in a queen's crown.

The sea king down here had been a widower for many years, but his old mother kept house for him; she was a wise woman, but proud of her ancestry, and therefore went about with twelve oysters on her tail; other distinguished persons were only allowed six. Otherwise she deserved much praise, particularly because she was so fond of the little sea princesses, her son's daughters. There were six of them, lovely children, but the youngest was the most beautiful of all. Her skin was as clear and pure as a rose petal, her eyes as blue as the deepest lake. But, just like all the others, she had no feet; her body ended in a fishtail.

All day long they could play down in the castle, in the large halls, where live flowers grew out of the walls. The big amber windows would be opened, and then the fishes would swim in to them, just the way swallows fly in to us when we open our windows; but the fishes swam right up to the little princesses, ate out of their hands and let themselves be patted.

Outside the palace was a big garden with crimson and dark blue trees; the fruit shone like gold and the flowers like a blazing fire, and their leaves and stalks were forever moving. The earth itself was the finest sand, but blue, like sulphur flames; over everything down here was a strangely blue sheen; it seemed almost as though one were high up in the air, and could only see the sky above and below, rather than on the bottom of the sea. In a dead calm one could make out the sun, like a purple flower from whose calyx all light streamed forth.

Each of the small princesses had her little patch in the garden where she could dig and plant just as she liked. One of them made her patch in the shape of a whale, another thought it nicer to have hers like a mermaid, but the youngest made hers completely round, like the sun, and only put in flowers that shone just as red. She was a peculiar child, quiet and thoughtful, and when her other sisters dressed up in the strangest things they found in the wrecks of ships, all she wanted, apart from her rose-red flowers, which looked like the sun far up there in the sky, was a beautiful marble statue of a lovely boy, hewn out of white, pure stone, come to rest on the bottom after a wreck. By the statue she planted a rose-

1 Vilhelm Pedersen, Denmark 1848
See List of Illustrations, page 63

red weeping willow; it grew splendidly and its fresh branches hung down over the statue, down towards the blue, sandy bottom, where its shadow appeared mauve and kept moving, just like the branches; it looked as though the top and the roots were playing at kissing each other.

Nothing gave her greater pleasure than to hear about the world of mortals up above; her old grandmother was obliged to tell her all she knew about ships and towns, human beings and animals; in particular she thought it strangely lovely that up on earth, flowers had scent (for they didn't at the bottom of the sea) and that the forests were green, and that the fishes to be seen amongst the branches could sing so loud and sweetly that it was a pleasure; it was the little birds her grandmother called fishes, otherwise they wouldn't have been able to understand her, for they had never seen a bird.

"When you reach the age of fifteen," said their grandmother, "you will be allowed to rise up out of the sea, sit on the rocks in the moonlight, and watch the big ships sailing past; and towns and forests, that's what you'll see!"

During the year that came, one of the sisters had her fifteenth birthday, but the others – well, each one was a year younger than the next, and so the youngest would have to wait five whole years before she might dare come up from the bottom of the sea and have a look at things in our world. But the one promised the next that she would relate what she had seen and found most lovely the first day; for their grandmother didn't tell them enough, and there was so much they wanted to know about.

None longed as much as the youngest, and she was the very one who had to wait the longest, and who was so quiet and thoughtful. Many a night she stood by the open window and looked up through the dark blue water, where the fishes swished their fins and tails. The moon and the stars she could see too, shining rather palely of course, but through the water they looked much bigger

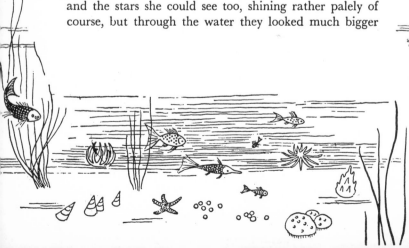

than they do to us; and if a sort of big black cloud slid along below them, then she knew it must either be a whale swimming over her, or else a ship full of human beings; they probably never thought there was a sweet little mermaid standing down below, stretching her white hands up towards the keel.

So now the eldest princess was fifteen and was allowed to go up to the surface.

When she came back she had a hundred things to tell, but the loveliest, she said, was to lie in the moonlight on a sandbank in the calm sea, close in by the shore, and watch the big city where the lights twinkled like a hundred stars, listen to the music, and to the noise and din of carriages and people, see the many church towers and spires, and hear how the bells rang; and just because she couldn't go up there, she longed for all this more than ever.

Oh, how the youngest sister listened! And afterwards, when she stood by the open window in the evenings, and looked up through the dark blue water, she thought about the big city with all its noise and din, and some-

2 Agi, Italy 1950.

3 Lorenz Frølich, Denmark 1837

times she thought she could hear the church bells ringing down to her.

The next year, the second sister was allowed up through the water to swim about wherever she liked. She came up just as the sun was setting, and that, she thought, was the loveliest sight. The whole sky had looked like gold, she said, and the clouds, well, their loveliness she just couldn't describe enough! Red and mauve, they had sailed along above her; but much faster than they, a flock of wild swans had flown, like a long white veil, over the water where the sun was setting; she swam towards it, but it sank, and the rosy glow on the surface of the sea and the clouds was extinguished.

The next year the third sister went up. She was the most daring of them all, and so she swam up a broad river that flowed into the sea. She saw lovely green hills covered with vines; castles and farms peeped forth from

26

4 *Yan' Dargent, France 1875*

splendid forests; she heard how all the birds sang, and the sun shone so warmly that she often had to dive below the surface to cool her burning face. In a little bay she came across a whole flock of little human children; they were running and splashing around in the water quite naked. She wanted to play with them, but they got frightened and ran off, and a little black animal came along; it was a dog, but she had never seen a dog before; it barked at her so terribly that she became afraid, and made for the open sea. But never could she forget the splendid forests, the green hills, and the lovely children who could swim around in the water even without any fishtails.

The fourth sister was not so bold. She stayed out in the middle of the wild sea, and said that was the loveliest of all; you could see for so many miles around, and the sky above was just like a great big glass bell. She had seen ships, but far away, looking like gulls. The dolphins were fun; they had turned somersaults, and the big whales had spouted water up out of their nostrils; it was as though there had been a hundred fountains all around.

Then came the fifth sister's turn; her birthday happened to be in winter, and so she saw what the others hadn't seen the first time. The sea looked quite green, and there were big icebergs swimming all around. Each looked like a pearl, she said, and yet they were much bigger than the church towers human beings built. They appeared in the strangest shapes and glittered like diamonds. She had sat on one of the biggest and all the sailing ships had been startled and sailed round the place where she was sitting with the wind flying through her long hair. But towards evening the sky had clouded over. There was thunder and lightning, and the black seas lifted the big icebergs aloft so that they shone in the bright flashes. All the ships reefed their sails; there was fear and trembling, but she sat calmly on her swimming iceberg and watched the blue streaks of lightning zig-zagging down into the shining sea.

The first time any one of the sisters came up to the surface she was always delighted with all the new and beautiful things she saw, but now, being grown-up girls and therefore allowed to come up whenever they pleased, they lost interest; they longed for their home again, and after a month they said that down below was where it was most beautiful after all, and that you felt so at home there.

Many an evening the five sisters would link arms and rise to the surface in a row; they had lovely voices, more beautiful than human beings, and whenever a storm was blowing up and they thought vessels might be wrecked, they swam along in front of the ships and sang beautifully about how lovely it was at the bottom of the sea, and asked the sailors not to be afraid of coming down;

28

5 *P. Bunin, Russia 1956*

but the sailors couldn't understand their words; they thought it was the storm, so they never had a chance of seeing the loveliness to be beheld down below either, for when the ship sank the human beings drowned and only arrived at the sea king's castle when they were dead.

So when the sisters, in the evenings, arm in arm, rose up through the sea, there stood their little sister all alone below, watching them go; she looked as though she were about to cry, but a mermaid has no tears, and so she suffers all the more.

"Oh, if only I were fifteen!" she said. "I know I should soon grow fond of the world up above and of the human beings who make their homes there!"

At last she was fifteen.

"Well, now we've done with you," said her grandmother, the old queen mother. "Come along, let me dress you up, just like your other sisters!" She put a wreath of white lilies about her hair, but each petal of the flower was the half of a pearl; and the old lady had eight big oysters clamped tightly on to the princess's tail, to show her high rank.

"It hurts so!" said the little mermaid.

"Yes, you must suffer a bit for finery!" said the old lady.

Oh! She would so like to have shaken off all this splendour and laid aside her heavy wreath; her red flowers in the garden suited her much better, but she didn't dare change. "Goodbye!" she said, and rose, light and clear as a bubble, up through the water.

The sun had just set as she raised her head above the sea, but all the clouds were still shining like roses and gold, and in the midst of the pale pink sky shone the evening star, bright and beautiful; the air was mild and fresh and the sea completely calm. There on the sea lay a big sailing-ship, a three-master, with but a single sail hoisted, for there was not a breath of wind and the sailors were sitting around in the rigging and on the spars. There was music and singing, and as the evening grew darker, hundreds of multi-coloured lights were lit; it seemed as though the flags of all nations were waving in the air. The little mermaid swam right up to the stateroom window, and every time the water lifted her up in the air she was able to look in through the crystal panes: there were ever so many people, all dressed up, but the handsomest of all really was the young prince there, with the big black eyes; he couldn't be much more than sixteen, and it was his birthday, which was the cause of all the festivity. The sailors were dancing up on deck, and when the young prince stepped out, over a hundred rockets rose into the air and shone as bright as day, so that the little mermaid became quite startled and dived down under water. But soon she poked her head out again, and then it seemed as though all the stars in the sky were falling down around her. Never before had she seen such magic with fire. Big suns whirled around,

6 *Falke Bang, Denmark 1955*

splendid fiery fish swung through the blue air, and everything was reflected in the clear, calm sea. It was so light on the ship itself you could see every single little rope, and of course all the people. Oh, how handsome the young prince was! And he went round shaking hands with everybody and laughing and smiling while the music sounded in the lovely night.

It had become late, but the little mermaid couldn't take her eyes off the ship and the lovely prince. The coloured lights were extinguished, rockets no longer soared into the air, and no more guns were heard. But deep down in the sea there was a rumbling and a roaring; meanwhile she sat on the water and rocked up and down so that she could look in through the stateroom window; but the ship sailed faster and faster, one sail billowed out after another, and now the waves grew bigger, huge clouds appeared, and in the distance there was lightning. Oh, there was going to be a dreadful storm! So the sailors reefed their sails, and the big ship rocked at a terrific speed through the wild sea; the water rose up like big black mountains as though they wanted to crash in over the masts, but the ship dived, just like a swan, down between the big waves and let herself be lifted again on the towering waters. The little mermaid just thought it was a nice trip, but the sailors didn't think so at all. The ship moaned and groaned, and her stout planks bulged at each heavy blow the waves hammered against her sides; the mast snapped in the middle like a reed and the ship floundered on its side as the water poured into the hold. The little mermaid could see now that they were in danger, in fact she herself had to be careful of the beams and bits of wreckage drifting on the surface. For a moment it was so pitch dark she couldn't see the slightest thing, but then there was a flash of lightning and everything became so bright she was able to recognize everybody on the ship; each fended for himself as best he could; she kept watching especially for the young prince, and she saw him, as the ship broke up, sink down into the deep sea. At first she was very pleased, for now he would be coming down to her. But then she remembered that human beings couldn't live in the water, and that he would not be able, unless he were dead, to come down to her father's palace. No, no, he mustn't die; and so she swam round amongst the beams and planks drifting in the sea, completely forgetting they might have crushed her. She dived down deep below the surface and came high up again between the waves, and finally she reached the young prince, who could hardly swim any longer in the stormy sea; his arms and legs were beginning to grow faint, and his beautiful eyes closed; he would surely have died had the little mermaid not come along. She held his head above water and then

7 *Mario Calandri, Italy 1947*

let the waves carry her with him wherever they wished.

In the morning the bad weather was over; not a shaving of the ship was to be seen. The sun rose up out of the water, ever so bright and red, and seemed to bring life to the prince's cheeks, but his eyes remained closed. The mermaid kissed his high, beautiful forehead and stroked back his wet hair; she thought he looked like the marble statue in her little garden, and kissed him again, and wished that he might live after all.

Now she saw land ahead of her: high, blue mountains on whose tops the white snow shone, as though swans were lying there. Down by the coast there were lovely green forests, and in front there was a church or a cloister, she didn't quite know which, but at all events it was a building. There were lemon and orange trees growing in the garden, and tall palm trees at the gates.

33

The sea formed a little bay here, completely calm, but very deep, right up to the rocks where the fine white sand had been washed up. In here she swam with the handsome prince; she laid him on the sand, and made particularly sure that his head was resting high in the warm sunshine.

And now the bells started ringing in the big white building, and many young girls came through the garden. So the little mermaid swam out behind some big rocks that were sticking up out of the water and put sea-foam on her hair and her breast, so that nobody should see her little face; and then she kept watch to see who might come to the poor prince.

It was not long before a young girl came along; she seemed very startled, but only for a moment, and then she fetched some more people, and the mermaid saw that the prince recovered and that he smiled at everybody round about. But he didn't smile at her out in the water; after all, he had no idea that she had rescued him. She felt so sad when he was led into the big building that she dived mournfully down into the water and made her way home to her father's palace.

She had always been quiet and thoughtful, but now she became even more so. Her sisters asked her what she had seen the first time she had been up above, but she didn't tell them anything.

Many an evening and morning she went up to where she had left the prince. She saw how the fruits of the garden ripened and were plucked, she saw how the snow melted on the high mountains, but she never saw the prince, and so she always returned home more unhappy than ever. Her only consolation was to sit in her little garden and put her arms around her beautiful marble statue, which resembled the prince; but she no longer took care of her flowers; they grew just like in a wilderness, out over the paths; they wove their long stalks and

34

8 Richard Bennett, USA 1938

9 G. Osterwald, Germany 1839

leaves in amongst the branches of the trees, so that the garden became quite dark.

At last she was unable to endure it any longer, but told one of her sisters about it, and so all the others immediately came to hear of it; but nobody else besides them and a couple of other mermaids, who didn't say a word except to their closest friends. One of them knew who the prince was; she had seen all the festivity aboard the ship too, knew where he came from, and where his kingdom lay.

"Come, little sister!" said the other princesses, and with their arms about each other's shoulders they rose up out of the sea in a long row just in front of where they knew the prince's palace was.

It had been built of a pale yellow, shiny kind of stone, and had big marble staircases, one of which went right down into the sea. Splendid gilded cupolas rose up over the roof, and between the pillars surrounding the whole building stood marble statues that seemed to be alive.

36

Through the clear glass of the tall windows you could see into the most splendid halls hung with costly silken draperies and tapestries, and all the walls were adorned with large paintings that were a real pleasure to behold. In the midst of the largest hall a big fountain was splashing; the water spouted high up towards the glass cupola in the ceiling through which the sun shone down on to the water and on to the lovely plants growing in the big pool.

Now she knew where he lived, and here she came many an evening and night on the water; she swam much closer to the shore than any of the others had dared, in fact she went right up the narrow canal beneath the splendid marble balcony, which cast a long shadow out over the water. Here she sat and watched the young prince, who thought he was all alone in the clear moonlight.

Many an evening she saw him sailing, to the accompaniment of music, in the splendid boat, with flags waving; she peered out between the green reeds, and if the wind caught up her long, white, silvery veil, and anybody saw it, they thought it was a swan lifting its wings.

Many a night, when the fishermen lay with their torches in the sea, she heard them saying ever such nice things about the young prince, and she was happy she had saved his life when he was drifting about half-dead upon the waves, and she thought how firmly his head had rested on her breast, and how fervently she had kissed him then; he knew nothing at all about it, and couldn't even dream about her.

Fonder and fonder did she grow of human beings, and more and more did she wish she might go and live amongst them. Their world, she thought, was much bigger than hers; after all, they were able to fly over the ocean in ships, climb high mountains up above the clouds, and the lands they owned stretched with woods and fields further than she could see. There was so much she would like to know, but her sisters couldn't answer all her questions, so she asked her old grandmother, and she knew a lot about the higher world, which was what she very rightly called the lands above the sea.

"If human beings don't drown," inquired the little mermaid, "then can they live for ever – don't they die like we do down here in the sea?"

"Oh yes," said the old lady, "they have to die too, and their lifetime is even much shorter than ours. We can live to be three hundred years, but when we cease to exist after that, we just become foam on the water; we don't even have a grave down here amongst our dear ones. We have no immortal souls, we are never given life again, we are just like the green reeds: once they have been cut they never grow green again! Human beings though, have a soul that lives on forever, goes

11 Zb. Rychlicki, Poland 1958

on living after the body has become earth; it rises up through the clear air, up to all the shining stars! Just as we rise up out of the sea to look at the land which belongs to human beings, they rise up to unknown, lovely places, which we shall never see."

"Why weren't we given immortal souls?" said the little mermaid sadly. "I'd give all my hundred years of lifetime just to be a human being for one day and thereafter have a share in the heavenly world!"

"You mustn't go thinking about that!" said the old lady. "We're much better off and much happier than those human beings up above!"

"So I'm going to die then, and float like foam on the sea, and not hear the music of the waves, see the lovely flowers and the red sun! Is there nothing at all I can do to get myself an immortal soul?"

"No," said the old lady. "Not unless a human being were to grow so fond of you that you became more to him than his father and mother; if all his thoughts and love were to be wrapped up in you, and if he were to get the priest to lay his right hand in yours with a promise to be faithful, now and for all time, then his soul would flow over into your body and you would be enabled to share in the happiness of human beings. He would give you a soul and yet keep his own. But that can never be! What we regard as lovely down here in the sea, namely your fishtail, is the very thing they find ugly up there on earth; they don't know any better; up there you have to have two clumsy posts called legs in order to be beautiful!"

Then the little mermaid sighed and looked at her fishtail unhappily.

"Let us be content," said the old lady. "We may hop and jump around as much as we like during the three hundred years we have to live in, and that is really time enough. Afterwards one can rest all the more con-

12 Ulla Sundin, Sweden 1954

tentedly in one's grave. This evening we are going to have a court ball!"

There really was splendour such as one never sees on earth! The walls and the ceiling in the big ballroom were of thick, but clear glass. Several hundred colossal mussel shells, rose-red and grass-green, stood in rows on either side and blazed with a blue burning flame that lit up the whole hall and shone out through the walls, lighting up the whole sea out there; you could see all the countless fish, great and small, that came swimming up to the glass wall; some of them had scales that shone a purplish-red, and others seemed to be silver and gold. Down through the middle of the hall flowed a broad, running stream, and on this, mermen and mermaids danced to their own lovely singing. Human beings on earth don't have such beautiful voices! The little mermaid sang most beautifully of all, and they clapped their hands at her, and for a moment she felt joy in her heart, for she knew that she had the most beautiful voice of all, on earth and in the sea. But soon she began thinking about the world above her again; she could not forget the handsome prince and her grief at not possessing, as he did, an immortal soul. And so she stole out of her father's palace while all the singing and festivity was going on within, and sat sadly in her little garden. Then she heard the sound of a horn floating down through the water, and she thought. "Now he's probably sailing along up there, the person I'm fonder of than father and mother, the person my thoughts are always with, and in whose hands I would like to place my life's happiness. Everything will I risk in order to win him and an immortal soul! While my sisters are dancing in there in my father's palace, I will go and see the sea-witch; I've always been so scared of her, but perhaps she can advise and help me!"

So the little mermaid went out of her garden, towards

42

13 Artist unknown, Japan 1922

the roaring maelstroms beyond which the witch lived.
She had never been this way before; there were no
flowers growing here, no sea grass, and nothing but the
bare, grey, sandy bottom stretching out towards the
maelstroms, which, like thundering millwheels, whirled
round, dragging everything they could seize hold of

down into the depths with them; she had to pass between these crushing whirlpools in order to enter the
sea-witch's district. Here, for a long way, there was no
path except across warm, bubbling mire which the witch
called her peat bog. Beyond it stood her house, in the
middle of a weird forest. All the trees and bushes were
polyps, half animal and half plant, looking like hun-
dred-headed snakes growing out of the earth; all their
branches were long, slimy arms, with fingers like writhing
worms, which moved, joint by joint, from their roots to
their outermost tips. Everything they were able to seize
hold of in the sea, they wound themselves tightly about,
and never released their grip. The little mermaid became
very frightened as she stood outside here; her heart
thumped with fear, and she was about to turn back.
But then she thought about the prince and the human
soul, and became bolder. She fastened her long, flowing
tresses about her head, so that the polyps should not be
able to grab her by them, folded her hands across her
breast, and flew off like that, the way fishes can fly
through the water, in between the horrible polyps, who
stretched their willowy arms and fingers out after her.
She saw how each of them had something it had seized;
a hundred small arms held whatever it was like strong
iron bands. Human beings who had perished in the sea
and sunk down here to the depths peered out as white
skeletons in the polyps' arms. Ships' rudders and chests
were held tightly, skeletons of land animals, and a little
mermaid whom they had caught and strangled; that
seemed to her about the most terrible thing.

She came now to a big, slimy clearing in the forest,
where big, fat water-snakes romped about and showed
their nasty, whitish-yellow bellies. In the middle of the
clearing a house had been erected of the bones of ship-
wrecked humans; there sat the sea-witch and let a toad
eat out of her mouth, just the way humans let a little

14 J. Leech, England 1846

canary eat sugar. She called the horrible, fat water-snakes her little chickens, and let them sprawl on her big, spongy breast.

"I know what you want all right!" said the sea-witch. "And it's very silly of you. Nevertheless, you shall have your way, for it will bring you into misery, my lovely princess. You want to be rid of your fishtail and instead have a couple of stumps to walk on, just like human beings, so that the young prince will fall in love with you, and then you'll be able to have him and an immortal soul as well!" At this, the witch laughed so loud and horribly that the toad and the snakes fell to the ground and sprawled there instead. "You've come just at the right time," said the witch. "After sunrise tomorrow I shouldn't be able to help you until another year were out. I'll make you a potion, and before the sun rises, you must swim with it to the land, sit on the shore and drink it. Then your tail will part and shrink into what humans call nice legs, but it will hurt, just as if a sharp sword were passing through you. All who behold you will say you are the loveliest human child they have ever seen! You will keep your gliding way of walking, and no dancer will be able to float along like you, but every step you take will be like treading on a knife sharp enough to cause your blood to flow. Do you want to suffer all this? For then I shall help you."

"Yes," said the little mermaid in a trembling voice, and thought of the prince, and of having an immortal soul.

"But remember," said the witch, "once you have taken on the shape of a human being, you will never be able to become a mermaid again. You will never be able to dive down through the water to your sisters and your father's palace, and if you fail to win the prince's love, so that he forgets his father and mother, thinks nothing but thoughts of you, and has the priest place your two

15 *Harry Clarke, England 1915*

hands in one another, that you may become man and wife, then you shall never have your immortal soul! The first morning after he has married another, your heart will break, and you will become foam on the water."

"I want to," said the little mermaid, and was as pale as death.

"But then you must pay me too!" said the witch, "and it is no small price I ask. You have the loveliest voice of all down here at the bottom of the sea, and you think you will be able to enchant him with it all right, but your voice is just what you have to give me. The best thing you possess, that's what I want for my precious potion! After all, I have to put my own blood into it, that it may become as sharp as a two-edged sword!"

"But if you take my voice," said the little mermaid, "what have I got left?"

"Your lovely figure," said the witch. "Your gliding walk and your eloquent eyes. You'll be able to enchant the heart of a human with them all right. Well, so you've lost courage! Come, stick out your little tongue so that I can cut it off for my payment, and then you shall have my powerful potion!"

"Let it be so," said the little mermaid, and the witch put on her cauldron in order to brew her potion. "Nothing like cleanliness!" she said as she scrubbed out the cauldron with snakes which she tied in a knot. Then she scratched her breast and let her black blood drip in; the steam took on the strangest shapes, enough to make anyone fear and tremble. The witch kept putting more things in and when it was boiling well it was just like a crocodile weeping. At last the potion was ready, and it looked like the clearest water!

"There you are," said the witch, and cut out the little mermaid's tongue, who thus became dumb, and could neither sing nor speak.

"If the polyps should seize you when you walk back

48

16 *Arnold Thornam, Norway 1926*

through my forest," said the witch, "then fling but a single drop of my potion over them, and their arms and fingers will burst into a thousand pieces!"

But the little mermaid had no need to; the polyps drew back from her in fright when they saw the shining drink that gleamed in her hand as though it were a glittering star. Thus she soon passed through the forest, the bog, and the roaring maelstroms.

She could see her father's palace, where the torches had been extinguished in the big ballroom; probably everybody was asleep now, but she didn't dare go in and see them, now that she was dumb and wanted to leave them for ever. It was as though her heart would have to break with grief. She stole into the garden, plucked one flower from each of her sister's flowerbeds, blew a thousand kisses from her fingertips towards the palace, and rose up through the dark blue sea.

The sun had not yet come forth as she saw the prince's castle and mounted the splendid marble staircase. The moon shone beautifully clear. The little mermaid drank the burning sharp potion, and it was as though a two-edged sword passed through her delicate body. She fainted from it, and lay as though dead. When the sun began to shine over the sea, she awoke, and felt a seering pain; but right before her stood the handsome young prince. He fastened his jet black eyes upon her, so that she cast her own down, whereupon she saw that her fishtail had gone and that she had the nicest little white legs any young girl could wish for. But she was quite naked, and therefore wrapped herself in her thick, long tresses. The prince asked who she was and how she had come there, and she looked at him gently, but sadly, with her dark blue eyes; after all, she couldn't talk. Then he took her by the hand and led her into the castle. At each step she took it was just as the witch had warned her, as though she were treading on pointed needles and sharp knives.

17 Vilhelm Pedersen, Denmark 1848

But she endured it gladly; she rose, light as a bubble, at the prince's side, and he and everybody else marvelled at her beautiful, floating walk.

She was given costly raiments of silk and muslin to wear, and in the palace she was the most beautiful of them all. But she was dumb, and could neither sing nor speak. Lovely slave-girls, clad in silk and gold, came forth and sang for the prince and his royal parents; one sang more beautifully than all the rest, and the prince clapped his hands and smiled at her; that made the little mermaid unhappy, for she knew she had once sung far more beautifully. She thought: "Oh, I would so like him to know that I, just to be with him, have given my voice away for ever and ever!"

The slave-girls now began to dance lovely, graceful dances to the most wonderful music, whereupon the little mermaid lifted up her beautiful white arms, rose upon tiptoe, and floated across the floor, dancing as none had ever danced before; at each movement her loveliness became more apparent, and her eyes appealed more fervently to the heart than the singing of the slaves.

Everybody was delighted, especially the prince, who called her his little foundling; and she danced on and on, even though every time her foot touched the ground it was as if she were treading on sharp knives. The prince said she was always to stay with him, and she was given permission to sleep on a velvet cushion outside his door.

He had a suit of man's clothing sewn for her, so that she could go riding with him. They rode through the sweet-smelling forests, and green branches knocked her shoulders, and the little birds sang in the fresh leaves. She went climbing with the prince up high mountains, and although her delicate feet bled so much that the others noticed it, she made light of it and went on with him until they saw the clouds sailing far below them, like a flock of birds setting out for foreign climes.

18 Torné Esquius, Spain 1918

At home, in the prince's castle, while the others were all asleep, she went out on to the broad marble staircase, for it cooled her burning feet to stand in the cold sea water; and she thought about the others down there in the depths.

One night her sisters came along, their arms linked. They were singing so mournfully as they swam over the water; she waved to them, and they recognized her, and told her how unhappy she had made them all. Every night after that they visited her; and one night, far out, she saw her old grandmother (who hadn't been up to the surface for many years) and the sea king, his crown on his head. They stretched out their hands towards her, but dared not come so close in to land as her sisters.

Day by day the prince grew fonder of her, and he loved her as one loves a good, sweet child. But as for making her his queen, the idea never occurred to him; and she would have to become his wife, otherwise she could never have an immortal soul, and on his wedding morning would become foam on the sea.

"Are you not fondest of me of them all?" is what the little mermaid's eyes seemed to say when he took her in his arms and kissed her beautiful brow.

"Yes, you are dearest to me," said the prince, "for you have the kindest heart of them all. You are most devoted to me, and you look like a young girl I once saw, but probably shall never find again. I was on a ship that wrecked, and the waves washed me ashore near a holy temple where there were several young girls serving, the youngest of whom found me on the shore and saved my life. I only saw her twice; she was the only one I could love in this world. But you look like her, in fact you almost supplant her image in my soul; she belongs to the holy temple, and that is why good fortune has sent you to me; never shall we part!"

"Oh dear, he doesn't realize it was I who saved his life," thought the little mermaid. "I carried him across the sea to the forest where the temple stands; I sat behind the foam and waited for somebody to come. I saw the beautiful girl of whom he is fonder than me!" And the mermaid sighed deeply; she couldn't manage tears. "The girl belongs to the holy temple, that is what he said; so she will never come out into the world, and they will never meet again. But I am with him, see him every day, will look after him, love him, lay down my life for him!"

But now the young prince is to marry, so people said, and take the neighbouring king's lovely daughter to wife. That is why he is fitting out such a splendid ship. The prince is going to have a look at the neighbouring king's country, that's what they say at any rate, but it is really to have a look at the neighbouring king's daughter, and he's going to take a big retinue with him. But the little mermaid shook her head and smiled, for she knew the prince's thoughts much better than all the rest. "I must go," he had said to her, "I have to go and see the beautiful princess, for my parents demand this of me; but force me to bring her home as my bride, that they will not do, for I cannot love her! She doesn't look like the beautiful girl in the temple the way you do; if I were to choose a bride, then I should rather choose you, my little dumb foundling, with those eloquent eyes of yours!" And he kissed her red mouth, played with her long hair, and laid his head against her heart, so that it began to dream of human happiness and an immortal soul.

"But you don't seem to be afraid of the sea, my dumb child!" he said as they stood on board the splendid ship that was to take him to the neighbouring king's country; and he told her about storms and calms, about strange fishes in the deep, and what divers had seen there, and she smiled at what he told her, for she knew better than anybody about the bottom of the sea.

During the clear, moonlight night, while everybody was sleeping except for the helmsman standing at the wheel, she sat by the ship's bulwarks and stared down through the clear water, and she thought she saw her father's palace; on the very top stood her old grandmother, her silver crown upon her head, looking up through the swirling currents towards the ship's keel. Then her sisters came up to the surface, gazed mournfully at her, and wrung their white hands. She waved to them, smiled, and wanted to tell them that all was well, and that she was happy, but the ship's boy came along, and her sisters dived down again, so he went on believing that the white something he had seen was foam on the sea.

19 Han K'ê,
China 1927

The next morning the ship sailed into the harbour of
the neighbouring king's splendid city. All the church
bells were ringing, trumpets sounded from the high
towers, and soldiers stood there with waving banners
and winking bayonets. There were festivities every day.
Balls and parties followed one upon another, but the
princess still had not arrived. She was being brought up
far away in a holy temple, they said, where she was
learning all the virtues of royalty. Finally she appeared.

The little mermaid stood watching eagerly to see her
beauty, and she had to admit she had never seen a more
lovely figure. Her complexion was so delicate and pure,
and from behind her long, dark eyelashes smiled a pair
of blue-black, faithful eyes.

"So it's you!" said the prince. "You who saved me as

I lay dying on the shore!" And he took his blushing bride in his arms. "Oh, I am much too happy!" he said to the little mermaid. "The best thing I ever dared wish for has come true! You must rejoice at my happiness, for you are fonder of me than all the rest." And the little mermaid kissed his hand, and she thought she could feel her heart breaking. His wedding-day would mean her death, and she would become foam on the sea.

All the church bells rang out, and the heralds rode through the streets and proclaimed the betrothal. On all altars scented oils burned in costly silver lamps. The priests swung their censers, and the bride and bridegroom held out their hands to each other and were given the bishop's blessing. The little mermaid stood there, clad in silk and gold, and held the bride's train, but her ears didn't hear the festive music, her eyes didn't see the holy ceremony, for she was thinking about her death-night, about all that she had lost in this world.

That very evening the bride and bridegroom went on board the ship; the guns roared, flags were flying everywhere, and amidships, a royal pavilion of gold and purple had been erected, filled with the loveliest cushions; this was where the bridal couple were to sleep all through the cool, quiet night.

The sails billowed in the wind and the ship glided away, easily and with hardly a ripple, across the clear water.

When darkness fell, multi-coloured lamps were lit and the sailors danced jolly dances up on deck. The little mermaid couldn't help thinking about the first time she had risen to the surface and seen the same splendour and joy, and she let herself be whirled into the dance, floating the way a swallow floats when pursued, and all cheered in admiration, for never had she danced so marvellously. It was as though sharp knives were cutting into her delicate feet, but she did not feel them; the pain cutting into her heart was greater. She knew that this was the last evening she would see him, the person for whom she had left her family and home, given away her lovely voice, and daily suffered endless torments without his having realized any of it. This was the last night she would breathe the same air as he, and gaze at the deep sea and the starry blue sky; an eternal night, empty of all thoughts and dreams was awaiting her, for she had no soul and could never have one. And there was joy and festivity on board the ship until long past midnight; she laughed and danced with thoughts of death in her heart. The prince kissed his lovely bride and she played with his black hair, and arm in arm they went to rest in the splendid pavilion.

All became hushed and still on board, the helmsman alone stood by the wheel, and the little mermaid laid her white arms on the bulwarks and watched for the dawn to appear in the east, for she knew that the first ray of sunshine would kill her. Then she saw her sisters rising up out of the sea; they were pale as she, and their long, beautiful hair no longer fluttered in the wind; it had been cut off.

"We have given it to the witch that she may bring help and save you from dying tonight! She has given us a knife. Look! Do you see how sharp it is? Before the sun rises you must thrust it into the prince's heart, and when his warm blood spatters over your feet, they will grow together into a fishtail, and you will become a mermaid again, be able to dive down into the water to us, and live your three hundred years before being transformed into dead, salt sea-foam. Hurry! He or you must die before the sun rises! Our old grandmother is mourning so much that her white hair has fallen out, just as ours fell to the old witch's scissors. Kill the prince and come back! Hurry, can you see the red stripe in the heavens? In a few minutes the sun will rise, and then

20 *Gerhart Kraaz, Germany 1959*

you will die!" And they heaved a strange, deep sigh, and sank into the waves.

The little mermaid drew aside the purple curtain before the pavilion and saw the lovely bride sleeping with her head on the prince's breast; she bent down and kissed him on his beautiful brow, looked at the sky, where the dawn was growing lighter and lighter, looked at the sharp knife, and fastened her gaze once more upon the prince, who in his dreams was calling his bride by name, for she alone was in his thoughts. And the knife trembled in the mermaid's hand – but then she threw it far out into the waves, and they shone red where it had fallen; it looked as though drops of blood were welling up out

59

of the water. Just once more did she gaze with half-glazed eyes upon the prince; then she leapt from the ship into the sea, and she felt her body being dissolved into foam.

The sun now rose up from the sea; its rays fell so mildly and warmly upon the deadly cold sea-foam, and the little mermaid felt no death; she saw the bright red sun, and high above her floated hundreds of transparent, lovely creatures; through them she could make out the ship's white sails and the red clouds in the sky, and their voices were music, but so ethereal that no human ear could hear them, nor could any earthly eye see them; wingless, they were borne through the air by their own lightness. The little mermaid saw that she had a body just like theirs, rising higher and higher out of the foam.

"To whom am I going?" she said, and her voice sounded like the voices of the rest, so ethereal that no earthly music could reproduce it.

"To the daughters of the air!" answered the others. "A mermaid has no immortal soul, and can never possess one unless she wins the love of a human being! Her eternal existence depends upon a foreign power. The daughters of the air do not have an eternal soul either, but they are able to create one for themselves by doing good deeds. We fly to hot countries where the warm, pestilential air kills people; there we bring cooling breezes. We spread the scent of the flowers through the air, bring refreshment and healing. When we have striven for three hundred years to do such good as we are able, then we are given an immortal soul and allowed to share in man's eternal happiness. Poor little mermaid! You have striven with all your heart for the same as we. You have suffered and endured, and have risen into the world of the air spirits; and now, by means of good deeds, you can create an immortal soul for yourself in three hundred years."

Arthur Rackham, England 1932

And the little mermaid lifted her smooth arms up towards God's sun, and for the first time she felt tears.

On board the ship there was noise and activity once more; she saw the prince with his beautiful bride, searching for her, sadly staring into the bubbling foam as though they knew she had cast herself into the waves. Invisibly, she kissed the bride's brow, smiled at him, and rose, together with the other children of the air, up on to a rose-red cloud that was sailing through the air.

"In three hundred years we shall glide, like this, into the Kingdom of God!"

"And we may be allowed in before too," whispered one of them. "Invisibly, we float into the houses of human beings, wherever there are children; for every day we find a good child, one that makes its parents happy and is deserving of their love, God will shorten our period of trial. The child never knows we are flying through its room, and if we smile with joy at it, a year is taken from the three hundred; but if we see a naughty child, one that is evil, then we must weep tears of sorrow, and each tear will add a day to our period of trial!"

22 Mario Calandri, Italy 1947

List of Illustrations

The blocks of Nos. 1, 3, 9 and 17 have been kindly lent by Foreningen Fremtiden (see No. 3). The other illustrations are reproduced from books in the Royal Library, Copenhagen (Nos. 13 and 18 from its Holger Laage-Petersen's H. C. Andersen Collection). Where the scale has been reduced, a number in brackets indicates the size of the original at its broadest point.

1: *Vilhelm Pedersen's* illustrations were published in Germany in 1848–49 and in Denmark in 1849–50 in a standard edition of all tales up to that date. The pencil drawings were reproduced in woodcut. Nowadays reproductions directly from the originals in the H. C. Andersen House are preferred.

2: Andersen: La Sirenetta. Ill. di *Agi*. Verona 1950, Arnoldo Mondadori Editore. (Each page 215 mm).

3: *Lorenz Frølich's* eleven pen and pencil drawings to the tale date from its year of publication, but were not published until 1955; the originals in the Danish State Museum of Art. See: Den lille Havfrue af HCA med Tegninger af *Lorenz Frølich,* udg. af Knud Hendriksen. Kbh. 1955, Foreningen Fremtiden.

4: Nouveaux Contes Danois, trad. par Ernest Grégoire & Louis Molland. Ill. de *Yan' Dargent*. Paris [1875], Garnier Frères.

5: HCA: Skazki e istorii. Ill. *P. Bunin*. Moscow 1956, Moskovskij rabočij.

6: HCA: Den lille Havfrue. Tegnet af *Falke Bang*. Kbh. 1955, Bianco Lunos Bogtrykkeri A-S, Bernh. Middelboes Reproduktions-Anstalt, and the artist. Same drawings in an Icelandic edition, 1947.

7: Andersen: L'ondina e altre novelle (Biblioteca del Mago Merlino). Ill. del pittore *Mario Calandri*. Torino [1947], Chianore. See also No. 22.

8: It's perfectly true and other stories by HCA. Transl. by Paul Leyssac. Ill. by *Richard Bennett*. New York, 1938, Harcourt, Brace & Co. (120 mm).

9: Mährchen und Erzählungen für Kinder von HCA. Aus dem Dänischen von Major [G.] v. Jenssen. Vignetten von *G. Osterwald*. Braunschweig 1839, Fr. Vieweg und Sohn. (125 mm).

10: HCA: Märchen. Eine Auswahl. Zeichnungen: *Werner Peltzer*. [Privately publ. by] Papierfabrik Schoeller & Hoesch GmbH, Gernsbach, Baden [1958].

11: J. Ch. Andersen: Bašnie. Ill. *Zb. Rychlicki*. Warszawa 1958, Nasza Księgarnia. (130 mm).

12: HCA: Sagor och historier II. I urval och övers. av Åke Holmberg. Ill. av *Ulla Sundin*. Stockholm 1954, Tidens Förlag.

13: [Andersen's Collected Tales] ed. by Norinosuke Morikawa. 3rd impr. Tokyo 1922, Shinju-Hakko. It is doubtful whether the illustrations were originally Japanese.

14: The Mermaid. From the Danish of HCA by Lady Duff-Gordon. With an ill. by *J. Leech*. In: Bentley's Miscellany Vol. XIX, London 1846.

15: Fairy Tales by HCA. Ill. by *Harry Clarke*. London &c. (George C. Harrap & Co.) and New York (Brentano's) 1915. (132 mm).

16: HCAs Eventyr I. På norsk ved J. Mørland. Ill. av *Arnold Thornam*. Oslo 1926, Mittet & Co. (126 mm).

17: *Vilhelm Pedersen*, see No. 1.

18: Contes d'Andersen. Trad. de Joan d'Albaflor. Ill. *Torné Esquius*. Barcelona 1918, Editorial Catalana.

19: HCA: Jen Yü Kung-Chu [The man-fish princess], ed. by Fan Chung-Yün. 6th ed. Ill. *Han K'ê*. Shanghai 1927.

20: Die schönsten Märchen von HCA. Aus dem Dänischen übertragen von Albrecht Leonhardt. Mit 243 Zeichnungen von *Gerhart Kraaz*. Gütersloh 1959, Sigbert Mohn Verlag.

21: Fairy Tales by Hans Andersen. Ill. by *Arthur Rackham*. London 1932, George C. Harrap & Co. (128 mm).

22: *Mario Calandri*, see No. 7.